Down Girl and Sit

Bad to the Bone

as a member of Exeter Public Library
Book Bunch

this book belongs to

Jacob

and rated it

→ 4 ←

thumbs-up out of 5

Bad to the Bone

by Lucy Nolan

Illustrations by Mike Reed

two lions

two lions

Text copyright © 2008 by Lucy Nolan
Illustrations copyright © 2008 by Marshall Cavendish
All rights reserved
Amazon Publishing
Attn: Amazon Children's Publishing
P.O. Box 400818
Las Vegas, NV 89140
www.amazon.com/amazonchildrenspublishing

Library of Congress Cataloging-in-Publication Data
Nolan, Lucy A.
Bad to the bone / by Lucy Nolan ; illustrated by Mike Reed. — 1st ed.
p. cm. — (Down Girl and Sit)
Summary: From the perspective of the dog, Down Girl, as she tells about her
days protecting her home from the enemy next door, Here Kitty Kitty, and the
many ways she tries to properly train her master, Rruff.
ISBN 978-0-7614-5834-0
[1. Dogs—Fiction. 2. Humorous stories.] I. Reed, Mike, 1951- ill.
II. Title.
PZ7.N688Bad 2008
[Fic]—dc22
2007030173

The illustrations were created in Corel Painter 8.

Book design by Vera Soki
Editor: Margery Cuyler

To Angelina, who loves dogs

—L.N.

To Jane, Alex, and Joe

—M.R.

Contents

Hamburger Man's house

Chapter 1

The Rug

Hello. My name is Down Girl and I don't like cats.

Some people think cats are cute, but CATS ARE NOT CUTE! Cats are dangerous. They stick to things. Squirrels stick to things, too. Just look up into the trees. They've got cats and squirrels stuck all over them. One could drop out of the sky at any moment. That's why I spend all my time protecting my master Rruff. I'm afraid if a cat or squirrel got stuck to him, he'd never get it off.

The worst cat in the world lives behind me. His name is Here Kitty Kitty. He sneaks into my yard and touches all my stuff.

You don't see me going into *his* yard and touching *his* things. Well, actually, I can't leave my yard. But that's not the point. The other day, I was sitting in Rruff's favorite chair. It was kind of lumpy. Maybe that's because Rruff was sitting in it, too.

I looked out the window and saw Here Kitty Kitty creeping through my backyard. I thought he might take my flowerpot, but no. He just rubbed against it and walked off. Next I thought he'd take my favorite stick. Instead, he stuck his nose on it. It is very sad to say, but Rruff didn't even notice. Rruff is a nice man, but he doesn't spend every second watching cats and squirrels. He's got a lot to learn.

I jumped against the window and barked and barked.

"Down, girl!" Rruff said.

"Rruff!" I answered.

"Down, girl!" Rruff said again.

"Rruff," I answered again. Rruff pushed me out of his lap and stood up. He walked into the kitchen and put a doughnut on the counter. Then he reached for a coffee mug. Only one doughnut? I wondered why Rruff didn't get one for himself, too.

I jumped up and took my doughnut.

"Down, girl!" Rruff cried.

Ah, he was calling me back for the coffee. Well, he should know I can't carry two things at once.

I ran to my little rug with my doughnut. But wait! My rug was gone! Here Kitty Kitty must have taken it! I didn't even see him come inside.

I dashed around the kitchen and Rruff started yelling. I was so upset I didn't feel like eating my doughnut. Well, okay, maybe I did. Maybe I would eat it under the couch.

Now I have forgotten my point.

Oh, yes. The rug.

It turned out that Rruff had put my rug in the washing machine. My rug used to be all stinky and hairy. When Rruff took it out of the machine, it smelled all fresh and rosy. It was ruined forever!

Rruff took my rug outside. He hung it up in the sunshine. He pointed at the rug. Then he wagged his finger at me. He spoke very sternly.

I think he was saying, "Don't let a cat take the rug." Then he went back inside.

I trotted to the fence to talk to my best friend Sit. We looked at the bright clean rug and shook our heads sadly.

"Some masters just can't be trained," Sit said.

"What should I do now?" I asked.

"Take a nap," Sit suggested.

Sit always comes up with the best ideas.

I crawled into my little house and fell asleep. I dreamed that I was chasing squirrels. I barked and woke myself up. My legs were still running. I was glad nobody was watching.

I lay back down for awhile. Suddenly, I had a weird feeling. I felt like something bad was about to happen. I looked out of my house. I could see Sit staring at something.

Sit was staring at Here Kitty Kitty. Not only was Here Kitty Kitty in my yard, he was heading for my rug! He reached out one paw and scratched it. Then he reached out another. Slowly, slowly, he dug his claws into the rug.

I crawled out of my house and snuck up behind him. I barked. Here Kitty Kitty jumped into the air. I grabbed the rug before Here Kitty Kitty could steal it.

There was only one problem. Here Kitty Kitty was stuck to it. I started running. I dragged the rug behind me. Here Kitty Kitty bounced along with it. I went under the picnic table, over a log, and around the shed.

Here Kitty Kitty went under the picnic table, over a log, and around the shed, too. I don't think he meant to.

What if he never came loose? What if Rruff just picked up the rug and put it back in the kitchen with that cat stuck to it?

I stopped and stared at Here Kitty Kitty. We were eye to eye. He hissed at me. And then it happened.

Suddenly, he puffed up. He was twice his usual size. He was going to explode! I was so startled, I shook the rug as hard as I could. Here Kitty Kitty let go. And on top of that, he flew! Not only was he a big puffy cat, he was a big puffy *flying* cat. He sailed over the fence and was gone.

9

Whoa! That was freaky. I looked at the rug. I shook it again and again to get the cat germs off. I ran through the mud and shook the rug again.

Suddenly, I realized Rruff was standing next to me.

I jumped up and wagged. Rruff looked at me. Then he looked at the muddy, dirty, hairy rug. He wrinkled his nose. Rats! It must still smell like cat.

Well, maybe this would be a lesson to Rruff.

I know *I* learned something new. I learned that cats can explode. They might even be able to fly.

But Rruff didn't learn a thing.

He washed the rug again.

Chapter 2

Bad to the Bone

Dogs are not like cats. We don't do bad things. And we certainly don't explode.

It is very easy for dogs to be good. That's because it doesn't take much to make us happy.

Dogs need only two things in life. Food and attention. Rruff should understand that. He needs lots of attention, too. Whenever I want to nap alone on the living room sofa, Rruff calls to me. "Down, girl!"

I wish Rruff weren't so needy. Other than that, he's a pretty good master. So I really don't know what got into him last week. It all started when he invited Sit's master over to paint the house. Sit came, too. We ran around the yard together while our masters painted. They were so busy, they never stopped to play with us. When

it got dark, Sit and her master went home.
I was still ready to play, but Rruff was ready
to go to bed. I tried to show Rruff we could
have a tug-of-war with the blanket. It is
hard to have a tug-of-war with somebody
who is asleep.

Rruff wasn't giving me any attention,
and I felt cranky. The next morning, I
talked to Sit about it. She wasn't getting
much attention from her master, either.

"Maybe we need to be bad," I said. "Bad
to the bone."

"It's worth a try," Sit said. "Surely our
masters will notice us then."

At first, we were not sure what to do. We had never misbehaved before.

On our morning walk, we turned to our friend Hush for advice. He seemed pleased that we asked.

"Well," Hush said, "there are several advanced moves I can suggest. They involve chewing and digging. But since you're beginners, I suggest you simply try a Snatch and Run. Just make sure that whatever you snatch is very important to your masters."

That evening, while our masters painted, Sit and I looked around the yard.

Ah, there was a tennis ball I had never seen before. It was brand new. "Wow, it must be worth a fortune!" Sit said.

I snatched it and ran. I looked over my shoulder at Rruff. Nothing.

I ran past him and looked over my shoulder again. Nothing.

I ran past him one more time and looked over my shoulder. *Wham!*

That's when I remembered you should

always look in front of you. Those trees will
get you every time.

It was obvious Rruff did not care about the tennis ball. I would have to find something even more important. I saw the stone elf. Rruff loves that thing. He's a very strange man.

I grabbed the elf and ran.

Well, actually, I didn't get it very far off the ground. In fact, I couldn't get it off the ground at all. I tried to run anyway.

Rruff didn't try to stop me. Maybe that's because I wasn't going anywhere.

Being bad was harder than it looked, but I gave it one more try. I looked around for the most important thing in the yard and, suddenly, I saw it. A pinecone! Rruff loves pinecones! He is always picking them up and putting them in a bag. I waited until I caught Rruff's eye. Then I grabbed the pinecone and ran.

Rruff still didn't chase me. I couldn't believe it. Okay, this was serious. I didn't want to do it, but Rruff left me no choice. It was time for Advanced Move #1. That's right. I chewed the pinecone.

Rruff did not care.

Boy, was he going to be sorry now. I was going straight for Advanced Move #2. I dug a hole and looked at Rruff. *You don't think I'll do this! But I will!* And I did. I buried the pinecone. I dropped it in the hole and covered it up!

Rruff didn't even stop painting.

I gave up.

Sit and I didn't know what to do next. We lay down and watched our masters. Finally, they climbed down from the ladders and went into the house.

Boy, they sure did leave a mess! They left their paintbrushes out in the open where any passing squirrel could steal them.

Sit and I decided to move the paintbrushes. Sit got one of them. I put my paws on the ladder so I could get the other.

Just then, our masters came back out.

"Down, girl!" Rruff called.

The ladder wobbled and the paint can fell. But at least I saved the paintbrush. I ran to Rruff and jumped up to show him.

"Down, girl!" he cried.

I think he was excited that I got paint on his shirt. After all, he liked the color well enough to cover our entire house with it.

Sit came running, too. We were more than happy to give our masters the attention they wanted.

Our masters' hands were full. They plunked what they were carrying on the picnic table. Then they grabbed the paintbrushes from us.

Sit and I looked to see what they had brought us. Iced tea is our favorite! We climbed onto the picnic table to sniff the box. Pizza! We couldn't believe it. "Down, girl!"

Our masters dove toward us.

Not only did they bring us food, now they wanted to play, too.

We grabbed the pizza box and ran. They chased us. We ran behind the shed. They chased us. We ran along the fence. They chased us. We ran all over the yard. We could have played forever, but our masters finally got tired.

21

Sit and I took the box into my little house and shared the pizza. Or most of it, anyway. We had dropped one piece on the ground, but we decided to leave it for our masters.

Oddly enough, they did not want it. So we ate it, too. We would have thanked our masters, but they had already gone into the house.

Here's the thing about masters. You just have to be patient with them. They did give us food and attention. All we had to do was wait for it.

Chapter 3

Sit Sat

I don't know where Rruff goes every morning when he leaves the house. I just know that he is very lucky that I stay home. If I goofed off as much as he does, the squirrels would take over. Sit and I are not about to let that happen.

We want to make the neighborhood safe for everyone—even the man next door. He is not my favorite person. He grills hamburgers in his yard and never gives me any. But I don't hold that against him.

Well, not much.

The squirrels in his yard are just as ugly as the squirrels in my yard. As far as I'm concerned, they all need to go!

Sit and I spend all day chasing squirrels. And, of course, we have Here Kitty Kitty to worry about, too. He has been sneaking around our trash cans again. He tries to get at all the wonderful things our masters hide in them.

We are very busy until our masters come home. Then we go inside with them. "Do you really think that is a good plan?" I asked Sit the other day. "How can our masters get a good night's rest, knowing we aren't guarding the backyards?"

Sit agreed that I had a point. The next day, we told Hush our worries.

"Hmm," Hush said. "Maybe we should all sleep outside."

"That's a great idea," I said. "Let's try it tonight."

Around three in the morning, I woke up Rruff so he would let me out. That way, I could protect him while he slept. It made sense at the time.

I went to the fence and looked across the street. I called to Hush to see if he was up. He called back to me from behind his gate.

Sit came to her fence. She said hello to both of us.

Then another dog said hello from down the street. I think it was that old bulldog.

He likes to stick his nose into everybody else's business. Or he would, if he had a bigger nose. His nose isn't big enough to do much of anything. And it makes funny noises, too.

But I have gotten off the subject.

Hush and Sit and I each walked around our yards. Everything was quiet. We came back to the gate and checked in. We didn't know what to do next, so we checked in again.

Our three voices sounded nice together. So we started to sing. It was kind of fun being the only ones awake.

Except we weren't the only ones awake. I could see the hamburger man through his window. He picked up his telephone. Then I heard our phone ring. Didn't he know he was going to wake up Rruff? Rruff came to the door. "Hush," he said.

Oh, no! He couldn't remember who I was.

I needed to shake some sense into him. So I ran over and jumped on him.

"Down, girl!"

Much better.

Rruff yanked me inside. Sheesh! I hadn't been outside that long and he already missed me.

The next night, Sit and I checked in with each other. Hush reported from his yard. The bulldog chimed in again. So did the hamburger man.

Rruff came to the door. He insisted that I come inside with him. I didn't want to leave my post. On the other hand, it's always nice to be wanted.

The next evening, I was in for a pleasant surprise. Sit and her master came over. We were all going for a walk. Instead of our usual route, though, we ended up at the park.

The park is an excellent place to chase squirrels. But our masters didn't want to. They walked us to a big grassy area, away from all the trees. Even better! There were all kinds of dogs standing in line. And there was Hush! We went to stand next to him.

"Sit," Rruff said. Sit walked over to him.

Rruff ignored her. That was kind of rude.

"Sit," he said again. He looked at me.

Uh-oh. He was getting confused again. So I jumped on him.

"Rruff!" I said.

"Down, girl!" he said.

Whew! He does know who I am.

A young man stood in front of the group. He talked for a while, then he walked over to us.

"Sit," he said. Sit walked over to him.

Sit was a very popular dog that day.

"Sit," he repeated, looking at me.

Sit sat. I wagged. Hush barked.

The young man stepped even closer to me. "Sit!" he repeated.

I jumped. Sit stood. Hush barked.

"Hush!" he said.

Hush wagged. Sit sat. I barked.

He looked at me again. "Sit!" he said.

Okay, this was getting ridiculous. Someone needed to tell him my name. I looked at my master.

"Rruff!" I said.

"Hush!" Rruff answered.

Oh, good grief.

Hush wagged. Sit barked. I sat.

"Good girl!" the young man said and patted my head.

That was not my name, but it was close enough.

The young man talked while our masters listened closely to everything he said. Finally, he blew a whistle. We all walked in a circle.

The young man held up his hand. We all stopped.

Ah, I was starting to understand. This man was a teacher. He was teaching our masters how to behave.

Well, good luck with that. They were all going to get an A in Walking Nicely. They were going to get a very bad grade in Remembering Your Dog's Name.

"Stay," Rruff said.

Who?

I looked at him and blinked.

"Stay." This time it was Sit's master who spoke. Sit and I looked at each other. Here we go again.

Our masters walked away. We followed them.

"Stay!" they shouted. An Irish setter barked.

Ah, that must be Stay. Sit and I went to say hello.

"Sit!" our masters said.

Sit and I gave up. We decided to just sit down until our masters started behaving.

35

"Good girls," the teacher said.

I rolled my eyes. This could have gone on forever, but thank goodness a squirrel ran past. We all jumped. We barked and tried to chase him. Our masters yanked on our leashes.

"Down, girl!" "Sit!" "Hush!"

Finally! They got our names right. Now they might pass the class.

We looked to see if the teacher was smiling. He was not.

Well, I can't blame him. We have been working with our masters for a long time. We haven't gotten very far with them either.

I wanted the teacher to cheer up, so I jumped up and kissed him.

"Down, girl!" he said.

Yes!

I wagged. It is very, very hard to train a human. But sometimes, just sometimes, they can surprise you.

Chapter 4

Rruff Learns a Lesson

I think that I have been trying to train Rruff the wrong way. I think I need to use more treats. It's hard to know what to give him. He has such odd tastes.

In the past, I have brought him a lizard and a stick and an old rope. He has thrown them all back outside.

Then I remembered the pinecone I buried the other day. I knew Rruff would like to have that for his collection.

So, I dug it up. Only it wasn't where I thought it was.

It must be over by the tree. I dug another hole. Nope, not there either.

I dug in front of the shed. I dug by the bushes. I dug and dug and dug. I couldn't find that pinecone anywhere.

However, I did find part of a garden hose. And a chewed-up glove.

When Rruff came outside, he saw all the holes. Then he looked at the garden hose and the glove. He was not happy. I guess he really wanted that pinecone.

Maybe that's what made him misbehave later. He did something so horrible this afternoon, I couldn't believe it. Here's what happened . . .

When Rruff came home, I was chasing squirrels.

Okay, I was thinking about chasing squirrels.

Okay, I was actually taking a nap.

But I still heard the car pull up. So I went to the gate to watch.

I couldn't believe what I saw! Here Kitty Kitty was lying on the sidewalk. How did I miss that? But here's something even worse—Rruff petted him!

Yes, he did. He reached down and scratched him behind the ears. Oh, where did I go wrong? How could I have raised my master to be so bad?

I needed to find that pinecone fast! I looked around the yard. Where did I bury it? Where hadn't I looked yet? Ah, I hadn't dug by the fence.

I had just started a new hole, when I heard the hamburger man come out of his house. I stood on my hind legs. I looked over the fence and barked. The hamburger man did not bark back. I don't think he likes it when I say hello. I don't think he even likes it when I look at him.

So I pretended I wasn't looking at him. Or his hamburgers.

The hamburger man put some hamburgers on the grill. The smell was too good to be true. I would do almost anything for one of those hamburgers.

Hey! Maybe Rruff would do almost anything for one of those hamburgers, too. I thought, *If I used a hamburger as a treat, I bet I could really teach Rruff how to behave.*

The hamburger man finished cooking the hamburgers. He put them on the table and went inside.

I looked down. As it turned out, while my brain had been thinking, my feet had kept digging. I had a pretty good hole going. If I wasn't careful, I would dig right under the fence.

I would end up in the hamburger man's yard.

I would end up right by that plate of hamburgers.

Right by that plate of big, juicy hamburgers.

Whoa! I was already there. How did that happen?

The hamburgers looked even better up close. But would they be good enough for Rruff? I needed to find out.

I ate a hamburger. For Rruff, of course. I thought it was pretty tasty, but just to make sure, I ate one more.

Or maybe it was seven.

Suddenly, the hamburger man came out of the house. He started shouting. Well, if he didn't want me to come over, he shouldn't have invited me. And believe me. If you set down food and walk away, that's the same thing as inviting a dog to eat it.

The hamburger man was shouting so loud that Rruff came out of our house. Rruff saw me and ran for the gate.

When he rushed into the hamburger man's yard, the hamburger man pointed at the hole. I think he was telling Rruff it would have been faster if he had come under the fence.

Rruff snapped a leash on me and shook his head. It was a very quiet walk home. It was so quiet, in fact, we could hear something rustling. We walked to the other side of the house.

The lid was off the trash can. Trash was flying up in the air.

Rruff leaned over the can. "Scat!"

Here Kitty Kitty flew out of the can.
He puffed up to twice his size!

Bang!

He finally blew!

I dove. I tried to take Rruff with me,
but he stood his ground.

"Shoo!" Rruff was shouting.

I uncovered my eyes. Here Kitty Kitty
hadn't exploded after all. That noise was
just the trash can falling.

Rruff was jumping up and down. And Here Kitty Kitty was stuck to his sweater!

I knew this would happen one day. It was horrible! It was terrible! And, honestly, it was downright embarrassing. I couldn't let Rruff go out in public like this.

I jumped up and barked right in Here Kitty Kitty's ear. He flew into the air. Rruff waved his arms and shouted. Here Kitty Kitty took off.

Quite frankly, I would have, too. Rruff looked like a crazy person.

Rruff looked at the trash lying on the ground. He did not smile.

Finally, he sighed. Then he scratched me behind my ears. I think he actually learned something today.

Cats are bad. Dogs are good.

I was very proud of Rruff. I looked at the stinky sandwiches and the soggy cereal lying in front of me.

Ah!

At least I could still give him a nice treat.

Smarter Than Squirrels
(Book # 1)

🎀 *A Gryphon Honor Book*
🎀 *Maryland Blue Crab Award for Young Readers*

"In a clever take on the dog story, this chapter book is told from the point of view of two canines who think they have a handle on the human world, but are amusingly mistaken. Shaggy Down Girl and spotted Sit laugh at their owners for not burying their treasures, and Down Girl protects all the food in the house by eating it. The snappy text mimics a yip-yappy dog's world, often frenetic and frantic, and full of well-intentioned mistakes . . ."
— *Booklist*

"Lively, expressive black-and-white illustrations shot from a canine point-of-view animate Down Girl's hilarious first-person narrative. This donut-loving

dog, with her unusual perspective, is sure to tickle all lovers of man's best friend."
— *Kirkus Reviews*

"In brief chapters, a pet dog describes how she guards her backyard against dangerous squirrels and thieving birds and chats through the fence with her canine neighbor, Sit. . . . Down Girl continually maintains that dogs don't lie, have big brains, and know how to protect their owners. Reed's humorous black-and-white illustrations add to the charm of this transitional chapter book by showing the human's frustration in dealing with his sometimes naughty, but always well-meaning dog. Animal lovers will enjoy this offering." — *School Library Journal*

★ "This will make dog lovers sit up and beg, and even reluctant readers, if tempted with a booktalk or chapter readaloud, will go fetch." — *Bulletin of the Center for Children's Books*, starred review

On the Road
(Book # 2)

🎗 A Texas Bluebonnet Award winner

"There's a whole lot of skill development going on here, but the stories are so much doggone fun, readers won't even notice." — *The Horn Book*

"Narrated from a dog's point of view, this easy chapter book covers the hilarious antics of two canine friends who puzzle through and explain life with their masters. Anyone who has owned a dog can relate to these tales. Children will be delightfully challenged by the perspective and ask for more." — *School Library Journal*

"Down Girl and Sit are best friends. They are also dogs, dogs who enjoy the finer things of canine life, including chasing squirrels, bothering their masters and eating crumbs. The charming first-canine point of view really works here—partly because Nolan keeps her dog's voice steady and humorous, and partly because she really seems to think like a dog. . . . Kids will want to curl up with their best friend and laugh at the adventures of Down Girl and Sit." — *Kirkus Reviews*